Seahorse was not a baby anymore.

He was on his own now.

And he wanted to see everything!

Seahorse swam away to a new place.

And there he found Cowfish.

Cowfish had two horns that came out
of its head!

Seahorse was happy to see Cowfish.

But he wanted to see more.

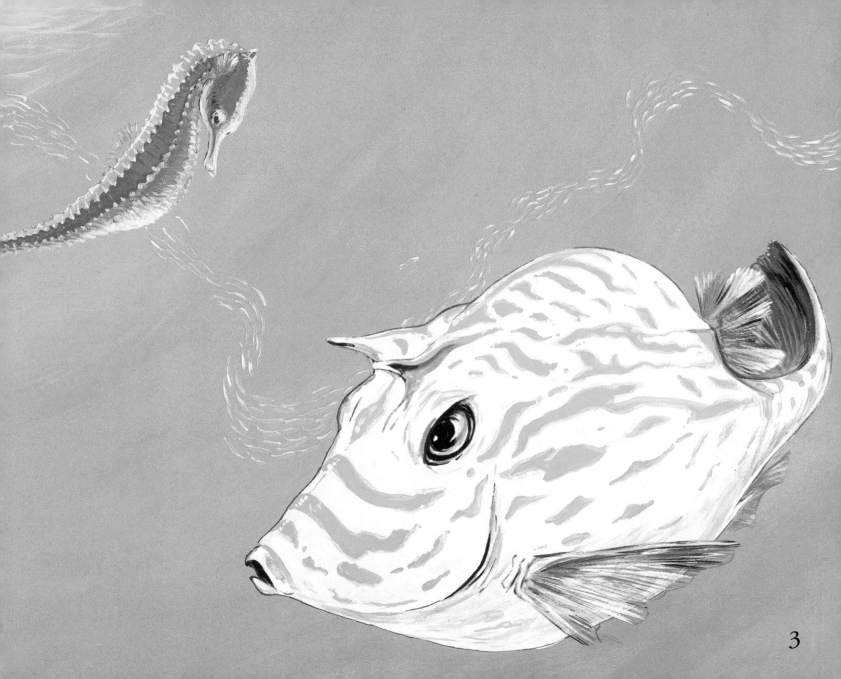

3

4

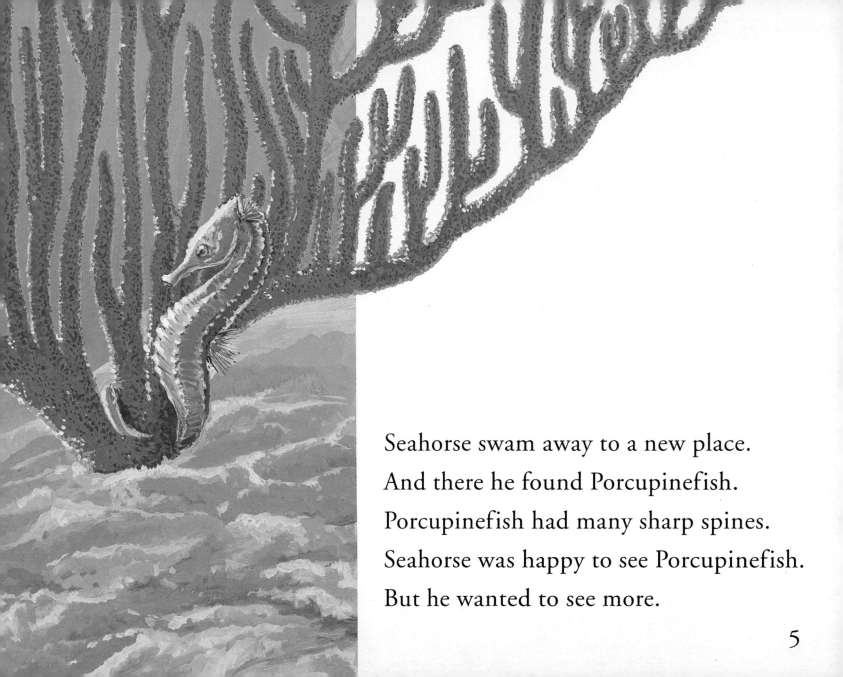

Seahorse swam away to a new place.
And there he found Porcupinefish.
Porcupinefish had many sharp spines.
Seahorse was happy to see Porcupinefish.
But he wanted to see more.

5

Seahorse swam away to a new place.

And there he found Dogfish.

Dogfish was a kind of shark.

Seahorse was happy to see Dogfish,

from far away!

But he wanted to see more.

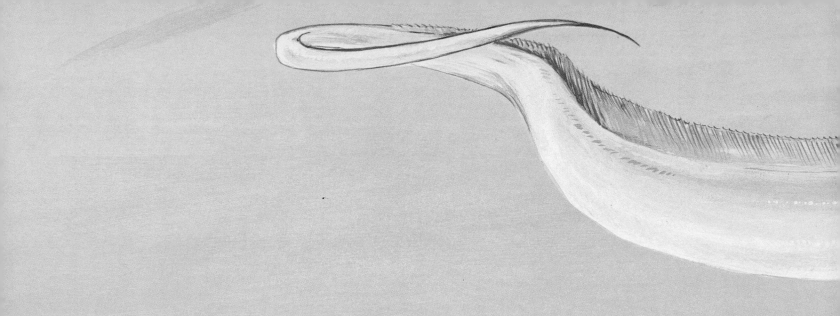

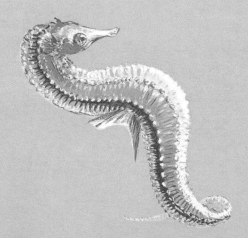

Seahorse swam away to a new place.

And there he found Ribbonfish.

Ribbonfish was very long and thin.

Seahorse was happy to see Ribbonfish.

But he wanted to see more.

Seahorse swam away to a new place.

And there he found Sawfish.

Part of its head looked like a saw!

Seahorse was happy to see Sawfish.

But he wanted to see more.

11

Seahorse swam away to a new place.

There he found Starfish.

It had five arms and looked just like a star!

Seahorse was happy to see Starfish.

But he was getting sleepy.

He wanted to go back to his own home.

13

Seahorse thought, "I'll make a wish on you, Starfish.
I wish I could find my way home."

Starfish turned one of her arms to the right.

"That must be the way home!" thought Seahorse.

"I think Starfish gave me my wish!"

When Seahorse got back home, he thought,
"I've had a great time, but I am glad to be home!"